Usborne First St

CINDERELLA

Retold by Heather Amery
Illustrated by Stephen Cartwright

Language Consultant: Betty Root
Reading and Language Information Centre
University of Reading, England

There is a little yellow duck to find on every page.

Once upon a time, there was a young girl called
Cinderella. She lived in a big house with her horrid
stepmother and her two nasty stepsisters. They all
hated her because she was pretty and because she
was always kind and good-tempered.

The horrid stepmother and nasty stepsisters made
Cinderella do all the work in the house. She worked
from early morning until late at night.

They gave her scraps of food to eat, old clothes
to wear, and made her sleep in a cold, creepy attic.

One day, Cinderella and the stepsisters received
invitations from the Prince to go to a Grand Ball at
the Palace. The stepsisters were very excited and
spent hours choosing new dresses, and buying
new shoes, bags and gloves.

When the great day came, they spent all day getting dressed and having their hair done. At last, when they were ready, Cinderella said, "Please may I come?" "Of course you can't. Stay in the kitchen," said the stepsisters, and off they went.

Cinderella sat down and cried. Then, suddenly, she
heard someone say, "What's the matter, my dear?"
She looked up and there was her fairy godmother.
"I wanted to go to the Ball," said Cinderella. "Do a
I tell you," said her godmother, "and you shall go."

"Now," she said, "bring me a big pumpkin from the garden, the cage with six white mice in it, the cage with a brown rat in it, and six green lizards from behind the water tub." Cinderella was very puzzled but she fetched everything as quickly as she could.

Then her godmother tapped each one with her magic wand. And, as Cinderella watched, the big pumpkin turned into a wonderful coach, the six white mice into six white horses, the rat into a coachman, and the lizards into six smart footmen.

Then her godmother tapped Cinderella's old clothes and old shoes with her wand. Suddenly, they turned into a beautiful dress and shining glass slippers. "Go to the Ball," she said, "but, remember, you must leave before the clock strikes midnight."

When Cinderella arrived at the Palace in her
coach, the Prince came out to meet her. Everyone
thought she was a Princess and even her stepsisters
did not recognise her. There was a grand supper
with lots of delicious food, and musicians playing.

The Prince danced with Cinderella all the evening
and she was so happy, she forgot all about the time.
Suddenly she heard the clock striking midnight.
"I must go," she cried, and ran quickly down the
stairs, losing one of her glass slippers on the way.

As she ran out of the Palace, the coach turned back into a pumpkin and her dress into her old clothes.

She ran all the way home in the dark and was sitting in the kitchen when her stepsisters came back. They told her all about the Ball and the strange Princess.

Next morning, the Prince was very unhappy. He wanted to find the Princess but he did not even know her name. All he had was her slipper. "I will search the kingdom for her," he said. "When I find the girl whose foot fits the slipper, she shall be my bride."

For days he went from house to house. Lots of girls tried on the slipper but it was too small for them. Then he came to Cinderella's house. The stepsisters tried to put it on. They pushed and pulled, cried and screamed but their feet were much too big.

Cinderella watched them. "May I try?" she said.
"No, you can't," shouted the stepsisters. "Let her
try," said the Prince. The slipper fitted perfectly. At
that moment, the fairy godmother appeared and
Cinderella's old clothes turned into a lovely dress.

"I have found you at last," said the Prince. "Will
you marry me?" "Oh, yes," said Cinderella. "Oh,
no," shouted the stepsisters, angrily. But soon the
Prince and Cinderella were married. They went to
live in the Palace and were happy ever after.

First published in 1988. Usborne Publishing Ltd, 20 Garrick Street, London WC2E 9BJ. © Usborne Publishing Ltd. 1988